THE SHADOW KNIGHT WARRIOR

Illusion of Time

By

James Cayo

"Four creatures from different periods of time fall victim to a time compression. In their dispersion to a lost world, they actively join forces to commence a missionary quest of finding their way back through time."

TABLE OF CONTENTS

BACKSTORY:

The Shadow Knight Warrior is a young hero chosen by the God of the Shadow Knights to embark on a vital mission, which is to restore time back in the lost world. Shadow Knight Warrior comes from a medieval period where he was born and grew up in a village called Golaam thousands of years ago before it was invaded by future droid time travellers. Shadow Knight Warrior grew up in a period when guardian forces controlled all portals and dictated the flow of time. Orphaned at birth, he was raised in a small, tight-knit community of monks. These monks had devoted their lives to protecting Golaam Village from the forces of evil that constantly sought to destroy it.

Early in Shadow Knight Warrior's life, he lost his family because of a time compression that yielded a shift in Golaam's portal; the cause of this time compression remained a mystery. The people of Golaam have been praying to the God of the Shadow Knights for a long period of time since the inauguration of the lost portal for a saviour. The answer to the prayers of Golaam has been the anointed birth of a young warrior of monk dynasty who is himself dispersed into a mysterious and isolated timeless portal where he finds himself alone.

Shadow Knight Warrior finds himself aloof and desperate in a shadowy portal with gloomy surroundings of cloud and dust. Once in a dream, the young warrior receives a divine revelation; the deity reveals to the young warrior a vision of a gigantic mischievous creature holding in its hands a shiny, luxurious gadget whose illumination disseminated symmetrically from the center; this gadget was conspicuously visible but latent outside of the centerpiece of Golaam. It was revelations like this that protruded trickery labyrinths of which the young warrior was to unleash for the sole acquisition of this nominal, ostensibly shiny gadget. As seen by the Shadow Knight Warrior, this gadget was precious in the sight of the creature and surrounding regime because of its universal dissemination and luminosity. Significantly, the young warrior perceived the impact this gadget had on all time and pathways, which were distorted due to the great mystery. After a series of revelations, the Shadow Knight Warrior is given an exposition about the vision by a revenant known as his grandfather; the revenant explains the vision to him that he had about the lost portal occupied by an evil genius known to have surreptitiously uncovered the secret of the portal's time and pathway.

The revenant reveals to him the name of the evil genius who grew up on an unknown planet thousands of years before its initial conception; the whereabouts of his origin are unknown, but it is said that he grew up intrinsically possessed with evil prowess derived from alien gods; it was the alien gods that endowed this evil genius with such ingenuity of unbelievable power. At the latter stages of life, this evil genius contrived super-intelligent entities that were stealthily equipped with self-contained magic and power. At 1000 years of age, this evil genius began unleashing labyrinths with the help of his droid servants to other portals and an extraordinary gadget that esoterically invoked time unto itself. It was this self-contained gadget that attracted the portals of Golaam and other places, which yielded the great mystery. After uncovering the secret portal of Golaam with the aid of a droid, the evil genius named his robotic servitor Ostraloid, who was to be his absolute servitor for the preservation of all portals, including those of Golaam. Due to his successful accomplishment, this evil genius began instructing over millions of droids, thereby earning the profound title of Professor K; this authority of the evil genius enabled him to reach a godly position that is unattainable by any other entity.

His droid servants have been partitioned and scattered abroad to conquer and fulfill the evil scheme of their master, which is the compression of all time. Out of all his droid servants, the most powerful one is Ostraloid who is one thousand years old. Altogether, Ostraloid and Professor K, whose real name is Balrioch serve as the main antagonist whose primary mission include the compression of all time.

After a long period wandering in the timeless portal, the young warrior encounters two vagabonds who, like him, were lost due to the time compression. One of them, named Attaka, comes from a fiery dense planet called Ashreke from a far distant time, which is filled with warriors, and the other, named Iceberge, comes from a cold and distant planet called Isiech from a time of the ice ages. These two vagabonds, Attaka and Iceberge, are from two different contrasting climates and the same period. Unlike the young warrior, these two men were taken from a time beyond the medieval period and were left abandoned in a wilderness before being compressed into this timeless and mysterious portal. The two men, including the young warrior, formed a posse known as the squadron. However, the squadron lacked resources for commodity, and it wasn't until the end of their inquiry that they found a passive droid lying on the dusty ground. This droid appeared to have suffered many periods of hunger and desolation. The squadron helped the droid rehabilitate. It was not until after the droid's recovery that he began speaking in a polymorphic tone that sounded anthropomorphically human. The droid was an indigenous of a far-distant place in the future called Humacon 16 that contained droids and cyborgs, and he was elected by the God of the Shadow Knights to assist the squadron in their divine mission.

Will their determination be enough to restore back time in
the lost world?

PRELUDE:

Time compression disrupts the fabric of space and time, pulling Shadow Knight Warrior and his world apart. As a result, he witnesses a space-time warp that isolates him from his family, who slowly diverge from his reach. Left alone, he is transported across an unknown space-time.

Before his awakening, the Shadow Knights—guardians of a place known as Golaam—are seen pleading desperately with their deities for immediate deliverance and a savior. This savior is a young man from a monk dynasty, chosen by the gods and cast into a timeless, isolated, and mysterious portal away from his village.

When the Shadow Knight Warrior awakens inside the dark, shadowy portal, he falls into a trance. In this state, he sees a vision of light from an unknown source. From within the light, he hears the voice of a god proclaiming his election as the chosen one destined to rescue a lost portal. After awakening from the trance, the Shadow Knight Warrior gropes through a dense cloud of shadows, moving in a single direction. As he trudges forward, he falls into another trance.

In this second vision, he sees a gigantic, mysterious creature holding an unknown gadget. The gadget radiates intense energy, its internal rays repelling space and time across every portal it connects to. It is powerful in the creature's hands, creating a series of mazes that link to other portals, rendering it both esoteric and evasive. Shadow Knight Warrior perceives the profound impact this gadget has on all spacetime regions. Surrounding the creature is an army of droids, aiding in the expansion of the maze and solidifying the creature's regime.

Suddenly, the Shadow Knight Warrior awakens from the vision, disoriented and struggling to decipher its meaning while searching for a way out of the unknown world. As he continues to follow the shadowy clouds, he unexpectedly encounters two vagabonds who, like him, have been transported to this timeless dimension.

The vagabonds, Attaka and Iceberge, hail from distinct and complementary dynasties. Attaka, a wild and avid wolf-hunter, is a master of the spearing windshield. He comes from Ashreke, a distant, hot, and dense planet filled with warriors and other humanoid creatures. Iceberge, on the other hand, is a half-human, half-cyborg being made of ice. He originates from Isiech, an isolated and frigid planet locked in the ice age. Both were affected by the same time compression and were chosen by the God of the Shadow Knights to aid in restoring the time and pathways of all portals.

Shadow Knight Warrior forms a bond with Attaka and Iceberge. Together, they begin their mission, but by default, Shadow Knight Warrior leads the group through the shadowy clouds until they stumble upon a droid lying dormant on the ground. When they attempt to assist it, the droid unexpectedly speaks in a polymorphic tone that sounds almost human.

The droid introduces itself as an inhabitant of Humacon 16, a far-distant planet. Like the others, it was a victim of time compression, which led to its arrival in the unknown world. The droid reveals it has been inactive for nearly a thousand years. Together, Shadow Knight Warrior, Attaka, Iceberge, and the droid form a band they call the squadron. United by their shared fate, they vow to escape the time warp and restore each of their worlds to their rightful place and time.

PROLOGUE

In the year 1270 AD, in the land of Golaam within the Shadow Knight Valley, a group of medieval Shadow Knights gathered at a sacred shrine. Their voices rose in songs of worship and prayer, a ritual passed down through generations.

In a nearby town within the village, a young man dreamed of following in the footsteps of his ancestors to become a Shadow Knight. He was devoted to his family, cherishing their legacy above all else.

At his home, the young Shadow Knight Warrior is dining with his father, stepmother, and younger sister—around a lively table.

"Father," the young man asks, looking up from his meal, "can you teach me how to pray?"

His father, the patron, nods solemnly. "Yes, son, I can teach you how to pray like a Shadow Knight."

"What is a Shadow Knight?" the young man asks curiously.

The patron smiles. "A Shadow Knight is what you were born to be. But it's more than that. Unless, of course, you wish to follow the path of a monk, like your forefathers."

The young man shakes his head. "I want to become a Shadow Knight Warrior."

"If that is your wish," his father replies, "then you must think like a warrior and learn the discipline of prayer. Always remember to pray, my son."

"Okay," the young man says eagerly, "but how?"

The patron begins to answer, but the moment is interrupted.

Above, the sky shifts. A strange, cosmic event begins to unfold in the heavens. The air grows heavy, and an unnatural energy descends upon the land.

Suddenly, a time compression strikes their zone. The surroundings bend and twist as though reality itself is being reshaped. The young Shadow Knight Warrior is torn from his family and dispersed to a different time and place.

Meanwhile, at the shrine, the Shadow Knights raise their voices in a desperate prayer for deliverance. Their words are spoken in an ancient, unknown tongue, echoing into the void.

CHAPTER 1
THE FIRST REVELATION

ShadowKnightWarrior jolted awake, gasping for breath. His chest heaved, and his hands clawed at the thick air around him, desperate to find something solid to anchor himself into. But all he felt was a heavy, oppressive emptiness. The world around him was cloaked in shadows, dense and unyielding, stretching into an endless void.

He felt like he was falling. But it took him some time to register that the feeling was something else. It was a mix of feelings, like one was falling and standing on solid footing at the same time. It took him a while to get used to this feeling.

"Where am I?" he murmured, his voice trembling as it echoed back to him in the darkness. "How did I get here?"

He tried to steady his breathing, but his mind raced. The last thing he remembered was sitting at the dining table with his family. His father's deep laughter still echoed in his ears, and the warmth of his stepmother's smile lingered in his memory. They had been eating together, the usual dinner. His younger sister had been teasing him about his dreams of becoming a Shadow Knight, though her teasing was always affectionate. It was all the same.

Had he taken it all for granted?

The thought of his family gave him a strange comfort, but it was fleeting. His surroundings were too alien, too ominous, to allow him to feel safe. He took a cautious step – or what seemed like a step – forward, but the ground beneath him felt insubstantial, as though he were walking on a mist that could vanish at any moment.

Suddenly, a brilliant light pierced through the oppressive darkness. It was blinding, forcing him to shield his eyes. The air around him seemed to hum with an otherworldly energy. Then, a voice rang out, deep and commanding, reverberating through the emptiness.

"You have been chosen," the voice declared.

Shadow Knight Warrior froze, his heart pounding in his chest. "Chosen?" he whispered, the word catching in his throat.

"Yes," the voice boomed again, its tone firm yet strangely calm. "You have been chosen to rescue a lost portal."

The words hung heavily in the air, pressing down on him like a weight he could not shake. His thoughts raced, trying to process the enormity of what he was hearing. "Why me?" he managed to ask, his voice barely above a whisper.

"You are the chosen one," the voice replied with finality.

The light began to fade, and as it did, so too did the voice. The silence that followed was deafening, leaving him alone once more in the oppressive void.

Suddenly, Shadow Knight Warrior jolted awake, as though roused from a deep sleep. He blinked rapidly, his eyes darting around. For a second, he felt a strange sense of comfort. Perhaps all of it was a dream. But as his eyes adjusted to the dim lighting, he realized that shadows were still surrounding him. "What? What could this mean?" he said aloud, his voice filled with awe and confusion.

He took a hesitant step forward, then another, his movements slow and deliberate. The shadows around him seemed to shift and swirl, as though alive, reacting to his presence. The air was thick, and every step felt like wading through a heavy fog.

As he walked, his thoughts drifted back to dinner with his family. His father had been teaching him the importance of prayer, a vital part of the Shadow Knight tradition. "A true warrior must learn to think like one," his father had said, his voice filled with wisdom. "But more than that, you must learn to pray. It will guide you when nothing else can."

At the time, he had only half-listened, more eager to talk about the legends of the Shadow Knights than to focus on his father's words. Now, in this strange, shadowy realm, those words came back to him with a new weight. Was this what his father had meant? Was this some kind of test?

As he continued through the shadowy expanse, a strange sensation washed over him. It started as a faint vibration in the air, then grew stronger, enveloping him completely. His body tensed, and his vision blurred. Before he could react, he was pulled into another trance.

In the vision, he saw a figure — a gigantic, mysterious creature holding an object that radiated an intense, almost blinding light. The object seemed to pulse with energy, its rays seemed to bend the very fabric of space and time. He could feel its power, its danger. The creature's form was shrouded in darkness, but its presence was undeniable, commanding the space around it.

Surrounding the creature were countless droids, their metallic forms gleaming under the light of the object. They moved with precision, their purpose clear as they worked to expand a labyrinth of mazes connected to other portals. The maze twisted and turned endlessly, a complex web that seemed impossible to navigate – intentionally impossible.

Shadow Knight Warrior's mind struggled to grasp the enormity of what he was seeing. He felt small, insignificant in the face of such power. Yet, there was a sense of urgency, a feeling that he was somehow connected to this vision, to this mysterious creature and its powerful object.

When he awakened, his legs wobbled, and he staggered forward, his mind spinning with questions. "What could this all mean? Is this real, or am I dreaming?" he muttered, his voice laced with doubt.

He pressed on, stumbling through the dense clouds of shadow. The weight of the visions bore down on him, and he couldn't shake the feeling that he was being watched, though by whom or what, he didn't know.

His thoughts returned once more to his family. He could see his stepmother's kind face, her gentle voice urging him to eat more. His sister's laughter echoed in his mind, teasing yet full of affection. And his father, always the steady presence, guiding him with wisdom and strength.

"I have to find a way back," he whispered to himself, the determination in his voice cutting through the fear. "I can't leave them behind."

But as he looked around, the shadows seemed endless, offering no clear path or direction. The sense of isolation was overwhelming, and doubt began to creep in. Was there even a way out of this place? Or was he doomed to wander these shadows forever?

Whatever lay ahead, he knew he couldn't stop. The voice had said he was chosen, and though he didn't understand why or what it meant, he felt an obligation to move forward.

With each step, the shadows seemed to grow thicker, the air heavier. But Shadow Knight Warrior kept walking, his thoughts a swirl of confusion, fear, and determination. He didn't know where the path would lead, but he knew he had to keep going. Whatever this place was, whatever purpose had brought him here, he would face it head-on.

CHAPTER 2
FORMATION OF THE SQUADRON

ShadowKnightWarrior trudged through the endless shadowy clouds, the silence pressing against his ears. Each step felt heavier than the last, and the strange, oppressive atmosphere seemed to sap his strength. How long had it been? Days, weeks, months? He had lost all sense of time, but his mind buzzed with unanswered questions about the vision and the voice that had declared him "the chosen one."

But how was he to figure the answers out? How was he to escape? There was nothing in this shadowy expanse. It felt as if it was sucking on the very essence of hope, depleting its prisoners of any chance of survival.

As he walked, a faint sound suddenly broke the stillness — a rustle followed by a soft crunch of footsteps. Shadow Knight Warrior froze. Someone — or something — was nearby. Initially, his heart leaped at the thought of another being in that strange, isolated space. But considering how strange it was in the first place, he did not know what to expect.

"Hey, who's there?" he called out, his voice echoing faintly.

From the shadows emerged two figures, their silhouettes outlined against the dim glow that seemed to emanate from nowhere. One was tall and broad-shouldered, with piercing eyes and a rugged demeanor. The other appeared lither and more angular, with a cold, calculating gaze.

Before he could react, he felt the cold steel of a blade inch close to his throat. The tall one spoke first, his voice gruff yet wary. "Who are you? "And where did you come from?" the other added, the one holding the blade to his throat, his tone sharp and demanding.

Shadow Knight Warrior raised his hands in a gesture of peace. "Wait, I thought I was alone in this strange place. I've been wandering, trying to find a way home. But then I had this vision — this strange, inexplicable ordeal. I… I don't even have the words to describe it."

The angular man nodded slowly, removing the blade from his throat. "You must have been affected by the same disaster as us."

"Disaster?" Shadow Knight Warrior asked, his voice tinged with both curiosity and dread.

The broad-shouldered figure stepped forward. "We don't know what it was. All we remember is being ripped from our worlds and thrown into this forsaken place. My name's Iceberge. I come from Isiech, a frozen planet of ice and stone. I was using my wristband to shoot ice — it's a skill passed down in my family — when suddenly, everything went black. When I woke up, I was here."

Shadow Knight Warrior stared at him, trying to process the revelation. "A frozen planet? That's rather peculiar. But… does that mean I'm not in my original time or place?"

The second man, who had been listening quietly, nodded. "You're not. None of us are." He extended his hand. "I'm Attaka. I hail from Ashreke, a scorching desert planet. I'm a wolf hunter by trade. Last I remember, I was in the middle of a hunt, tracking a pack through the dunes, when the ground seemed to collapse beneath me. And then… this."

Shadow Knight Warrior shook his hand, his mind reeling. He looked down, his heart aching. "Then it's true. I've lost my family." His voice cracked as he continued, "I loved them so much. I can't bear the thought of never seeing them again."

Iceberge placed a hand on Shadow Knight Warrior's shoulder. "You're not alone in this. We've all lost something — our homes, our families, everything we knew."

Attaka nodded in agreement. "We may not know why we're here, but we can figure it out together. No one should face this alone."

Their words brought a flicker of hope to Shadow Knight Warrior's heart. "Thank you," he said quietly.

As they sat together to rest, the three began to share more about their lives. Iceberge described the harsh beauty of Isiech, a world of perpetual frost where survival depended on cunning and resilience. "I was born with the ability to manipulate ice," he explained. "It's more than a skill — it's a part of who I am. But now, in this place, it feels useless."

Attaka spoke of the searing deserts of Ashreke, where hunters like him protected their villages from predatory wolf packs. "My people relied on us to keep the wolves at bay," he said, his voice heavy with regret. "I don't know what's happening to them now that I'm gone."

Shadow Knight Warrior shared his own story, recounting his upbringing in a monk dynasty. "My father always said I was destined for greatness," he admitted. "He taught me to think and pray like a warrior, to find strength in discipline and faith. But I never imagined it would come to this."

Iceberge leaned forward. "Shadow Knight Warrior, your father's teachings might be exactly what you need now. We're all out of our element here, but maybe this is our chance to prove ourselves."

Attaka grinned. "Besides, you're not alone anymore. We're a team now."

The words resonated with Shadow Knight Warrior. For the first time since arriving in this shadowy realm, he felt a glimmer of hope. "You're right," he said, his voice steady. "If I'm to live up to my father's vision, I can't give up now. We'll find a way out of this together."

The three stood, their resolve renewed. Iceberge extended a hand. "To the squadron?"

Attaka placed his hand on top of Iceberge's. "To the squadron."

Shadow Knight Warrior joined them, a small smile breaking through his somber expression. "To the squadron."

With their bond solidified, the newly formed team set off into the shadows, their determination burning brighter than ever. They didn't know what lay ahead, but they knew they had each other — and for now, that was enough.

Chapter 3
Escape from the Time Warp

The shadowy clouds thickened around the squadron as they moved cautiously forward. Every step was taken with caution. The space was vast and empty, and they did not wish to risk losing each other and finding themselves alone once again.

They didn't have the faintest clue as to where to go, but something about working together as a team made them feel that they would find their way towards something very soon, or so they thought. Shadow Knight Warrior led the group, his armor glinting faintly in the dim light. Behind him, Attaka scanned the surroundings with his spear-like windshield ready, and Iceberge followed, his armless band shimmering with a faint frost.

Suddenly, Iceberge stopped mid-step and pointed ahead.

"Wait," he said, his voice cutting through the silence. "Do you see that?"

Discovery of a Droid

Ahead of them, partially buried under a layer of ash-like dust, lay what appeared to be a humanoid figure. Its metallic surface gleamed faintly, and strange symbols adorned its chest plate.

The group approached cautiously.

"Wooooooooooooah," Attaka breathed, his voice filled with awe. "What is that?"

Shadow Knight Warrior crouched down, brushing away the dust with his gauntleted hand. "It looks like some kind of...alien."

Iceberge tilted his head, his icy demeanor giving way to curiosity. "Do you think it's alive?"

As Attaka leaned closer to it, and before anyone could respond, the figure's eyes flickered to life, glowing with a soft blue light. The squadron instantly jumped back, and their hands reached for their respective weapons instinctively.

The robot-like figure's body twitched, then rose smoothly to a sitting position. A mechanized voice emanated from it.

"Hello. Have you awakened me from my sleep? Please identify yourselves." It was definitely a robot of some sort; the voice was unmistakenly not human.

Shadow Knight Warrior stood, his hands shaking restlessly. "Sleep?" he repeated, baffled. "You're a machine. You can sleep?"

"I am not just a machine," the figure replied. "I am GNOBEPCI8, an assistive robot from the planet Humacon 16. And yes, I have been in a dormant state for over a thousand years. It seems like I have been compressed to a far distant past than my own since I am for the first time standing before you three who appear to be from a more human climate."

The squadron exchanged incredulous glances.

"Humacon 16?" Attaka asked. "Where's that?"

GNOBEPCI8's optical sensors flickered as it scanned the trio. "You are not from here, are you? This realm is a byproduct of a time compression. I, too, was displaced from my own era when the compression occurred."

"What do you mean by 'time compression'?" Shadow Knight Warrior asked, his voice sharp with urgency. "And is there a way to escape?"

The droid hesitated before answering. "Time compression is a rupture in temporal streams, forcing elements of different eras to converge. Escaping it is...complicated. But not impossible."

A glimmer of hope sparked in the group. Iceberge stepped forward. "Can you help us?"

"I can," GNOBEPCI8 said. "There is a portal nearby, but its location is obscured. If we work together, we may be able to find it."

"Welcome aboard, GNOBEPCI8," Shadow Knight Warrior said, offering a nod of approval. Attaka and Iceberge echoed the same sentiment. And just like that, the squadron now has a new member.

With GNOBEPCI8 now guiding them, they felt more confident as they moved deeper into the shadowy landscape. Eventually, they came upon a jagged opening in the ground. A faint glow emanated from within.

"What is that?" Attaka asked, peering into the fissure.

GNOBEPCI8 adjusted its sensors. "It appears to be a compendium — a repository of knowledge and tools. Let us investigate."

The group descended carefully into the opening. Inside, they found an array of items glowing faintly on pedestals. A vial of shimmering liquid sat beside a strange orb that seemed to contain swirling winds. A third pedestal held a crystalline object that pulsed with strange and shadowy energy.

"These must be important," Iceberge said, reaching for the crystalline object.

GNOBEPCI8 nodded. "The items represent elemental forces along with a shiny energy source. They will aid us in overcoming the challenges ahead."

As the squadron collected the items, Shadow Knight Warrior noticed something half-buried in the dirt. He knelt down and pulled out a sword, its blade gleaming with an ethereal light.

"A fallen sword," he murmured. "This feels...right."

He gripped the hilt, a sense of purpose surging through him. "This will help me fulfill my role as the chosen warrior."

Their journey continued until GNOBEPCI8 paused suddenly. Its sensors whirred, and it pointed toward a metallic device partially embedded in the ground.

"A holographic projector," it announced. "It may reveal the portal's location."

The droid activated the projector with a precise laser beam. The device hummed to life, casting a 3D image of a swirling, glowing portal into the air. The portal shimmered with energy, its edges cracked with light.

"What is that?" Attaka asked, shielding his eyes.

"A gateway," GNOBEPCI8 said. "It appears to lead to a point in the distant future."

The squadron moved closer to the portal, but before they could reach it, a sharp mechanical whirring filled the air. Out of the portal, a group of teleporting droids emerged, their forms sleek and menacing.

"Prepare for battle!" "GNOBEPCI8 commanded, and the Shadow Knight Warrior began drawing the hilt of his newly acquired sword"

Attaka readied his spearing windshield, and Iceberge activated his armless band. GNOBEPCI8 adjusted its laser beam actuator, its sensors locking onto the approaching enemies.

The enemy droids struck first, their movements rapid and disorienting. Shadow Knight Warrior blocked an incoming strike with his sword, countering with a powerful Shadow Attack that sent one droid flying backward.

Attaka lunged forward, his windshield spear slicing through another enemy. "These things are tough!" he shouted.

Iceberge unleashed a flurry of ice attacks, freezing one droid in place before shattering it with a Requiem Beam. "Keep them coming!" he taunted, his confidence growing.

GNOBEPCI8 provided support, firing precise laser beams that disabled the droids' mobility. When a droid attempted to flank the group, the droid's scrolling arm extended, smashing it into the ground.

The battle raged on, but the squadron fought with determination and synergy. One by one, the enemy droids fell until none remained.

As the dust settled, GNOBEPCI8 analyzed the portal again. "The path is clear. If we step through, we may reach a timeline closer to where we need to be."

Shadow Knight Warrior looked at his companions. "Ready?"

Attaka grinned. "Always."

Iceberge nodded. "Let's do this."

Together, the squadron stepped into the portal, leaving the shadowy terrain behind. The light enveloped them, and their next ordeal awaited.

Chapter 4
Journey to an Unknown Future

Stepping into the portal was like being swallowed by a mirage of light and sound. The squadron felt themselves stretched and compressed, as if the very fabric of space and time was folding around them. Their cries of alarm mixed with the eerie hum of the portal's energy.

"Whoooooooaahhh!" Shadow Knight Warrior clutched at the air, searching for anything solid to anchor himself.

Then, as quickly as it began, the chaos ceased. The squadron found themselves standing in an entirely unfamiliar landscape. The air was quiet and still, and the sky above shimmered with metallic hues. All around them were sleek buildings, their structures seemingly alive with an internal glow.

"Welcome to the future," a calm, mechanical voice greeted them.

The squadron turned to face GNOBEPCI8, who had emerged from a nearby structure. The droid's holographic projector lit up, scanning the area.

"What year is this?" Iceberge asked, his voice tinged with both curiosity and unease.

"I cannot decipher the exact time," GNOBEPCI8 replied. "The temporal distortion has disrupted my internal clock." The squadron's attention shifted to the world around them. The streets were devoid of human life, populated instead by droids gliding silently through the air. Teleportation chambers dotted the landscape, their energy fields pulsing rhythmically.

"This place… it's empty," Shadow Knight Warrior murmured.

"Not quite," GNOBEPCI8 corrected. "Flying droids patrol the area. They appear to be hostile."

As if on cue, a squadron of flying droids descended from the sky, their glowing eyes locking onto the intruders.

"Prepare yourselves!" GNOBEPCI8 shouted.

The battle was swift but intense. The squadron fought with synchronized precision; it seemed that just after one previous encounter, the squadron had managed to synchronize their battle movements according to each other. GNOBEPCI8, being technologically similar to the droids, helped the squadron eliminate them one by one. Laser beams and energy blasts lit up the area as they dismantled the droids, piece by piece.

When the dust settled, the team r egrouped near a teleportation chamber.

"Let's use this to move forward," Attaka suggested.

GNOBEPCI8 nodded. "It will transport us to another part of the time warp. However, our journey is far from over."

Squadron discovers unoccupied Base Portal

As they prepared to enter the chamber, GNOBEPCI8's sensors activated. A holographic map projected into the air, displaying a glowing dot several light-years away.

"I have detected an unoccupied portal," the droid announced. "It is three light-years from here and appears to be a deserted region. This portal may offer a temporary refuge while we work to restore the timeline."

"How long has it been unoccupied?" Iceberge inquired.

"Approximately 600 solar days, based on the data I've collected," GNOBEPCI8 replied. "It seems to have been displaced from another temporal period, causing its original inhabitants to vanish."

"How do we get there?" Shadow Knight Warrior asked.

"I will morph into a faster-than-light transporter," GNOBEPCI8 explained. "It is the only way to travel such a distance swiftly."

The team prepared for the journey, gathering their gear and remaining alert for enemy droids. Just as they were about to depart, GNOBEPCI8's sensors detected a nearby intrusion.

"Enemy droids are closing in!" the droid warned. "Follow me!"

The squadron evaded the approaching droids, weaving through narrow corridors and abandoned structures. Once they were clear, GNOBEPCI8 initiated his transformation. His metallic frame expanded and shifted, emitting a radiant glow as he morphed into a sleek, high-speed transporter.

"Climb aboard!" he commanded.

The squadron boarded the transporter, and in an instant, they were propelled across space-time. The journey was a blur of light and motion, unlike anything they had ever experienced.

When they finally emerged, they found themselves on a deserted island. The air was cool, and the ground beneath them was covered in shimmering particles of light. GNOBEPCI8 reverted to his original form, scanning the area.

"This island is uninhabited," he stated. "The light particles here may hold clues to its history."

The squadron followed GNOBEPCI8 as he traced the path of the particles. Their journey led them to a towering dome, its surface glinting like polished silver.

"Behold," GNOBEPCI8 announced, "a dome 8,000 feet in height. It appears to be desolate and uninhabitable, but it will serve as our retreat for now."

"Amen," Shadow Knight Warrior said with a faint smile. "Finally, a place to rest and pray."

"Is it warm inside?" Attaka asked, shivering slightly.

"The dome contains many accommodations," GNOBEPCI8 assured them. "Let us explore its interior."

The squadron cautiously stepped into the dome, their footsteps echoing in the vast emptiness. At the center of the space was a spherical bowl, its surface shimmering with faint light particles that danced like fireflies.

GNOBEPCI8 moved closer, his sensors emitting soft beeps as he analyzed the structure. His mechanical eyes sparkled with recognition.

GNOBEPCI8 constructs a Time Machine

"This spherical dome," he began, his voice echoing in the hollow chamber, "channels light particles from the outer region of the planet to send signals across interstellar distances. With this, I can construct a time machine to escape the time warp." At that moment, the squadron began exchanging hopeful glances.

As GNOBEPCI8 activated his holographic projector, a glowing map of the cosmic warp materialized in mid-air. He zoomed in on their location, pinpointing the dome's exact position on the mysterious planet.

"Here is where we are," he explained before shutting off the projection. "Now, let's begin."

GNOBEPCI8 worked with precision, harnessing the light particles emanating from the spherical bowl. Tiny sparks danced in the air as he assembled components, his movements fluid and deliberate. The squadron observed in silence, their minds drifting to thoughts of returning home.

Shadow Knight Warrior broke the silence first. "Before all this, I was with my family, sharing a meal. Then, in an instant, I felt myself being ripped apart, bent backward, and flung into this void. I'll never forget the terror of that moment — or the faces I left behind."

Attaka nodded solemnly. "I was hunting in the desert when it happened. Everything around me shattered like glass. I couldn't see anything but dust. I thought I was lost forever until I met you both."

Iceberge added, "I was gliding on glaciers, preparing for a tournament. Then, I was sucked into what felt like a vacuum, and when I landed here...it was nothing like home."

Their stories hung in the air, a shared pain that bonded them further.

As the light particles gravitated toward the upper vertex of the dome, GNOBEPCI8 paused. "I need to trace their origin. Wait here."

He launched himself upward, following the radiant beams that disappeared into the vertex. The squadron watched in awe as his silhouette grew smaller and smaller until it was gone.

Shadow Knight Warrior knelt down, his head bowed. "It's time for me to pray," he murmured.

Attaka and Iceberge exchanged glances before speaking. "Do you think your prayers will get us out of this?" Iceberge asked.

"No," Shadow Knight Warrior replied, his tone steady. "But they make me stronger. And strength is what I need to survive."

"Just remember this is not just your fight but our fight. We are in this together," Iceberge said.

In a moment of unity, the three put their fists together and knelt down to pray. Shadow Knight Warrior felt something powerful about this communal effort.

After what felt like hours, GNOBEPCI8 returned, a dazzling light trailing behind him. As he descended into the dome, the squadron stood in stunned silence.

The droid's voice broke the spell. "Behold, our new time machine."

The time machine was a marvel, its frame glowing with an otherworldly spectrum of colors. Light particles swirled within its core, guided by the intricate mechanisms GNOBEPCI8 had constructed.

Attaka couldn't contain his excitement, jumping up and down. "At last! At last!"

Shadow Knight Warrior sank to his knees, his hands raised toward the machine. "Finally, I can return home."

They didn't know what to expect from the next part of their journey, but knowing there was a way out made them rejoice with hope.

CHAPTER 5
JOURNEY TO THE PAST

The squadron stood at the edge of an incredible leap into history. GNOBEPCI8's metallic voice echoed across the chamber.

"We must ensure complete concealment before entering the time machine," the droid said, his mechanical hand adjusting the controls. With precise movements, GNOBEPCI8 set the time machine's destination to a staggering 1 million light-years away and 300.23 years back in time.

As the machine powered up, GNOBEPCI8 began to morph, his sleek body transforming into an advanced transporter. The squadron exchanged glances, a mix of awe and trepidation on their faces, before stepping inside.

Within moments, they were hurtling through the wormhole, surrounded by endless colors and faint outlines of primitive creatures. The journey was caliginous, their senses overwhelmed by the sheer magnitude of time and space bending around them.

Squadron lands in Mesozoic Era

When the transporter emerged on solid ground, the squadron felt a jarring tremor. They found themselves inside a cavern, the air heavy with the echoes of thunderous footsteps. Shadow Knight Warrior strained to listen.

"What... is that sound?" he asked, his voice uneasy.

"It's too loud," Iceberge said, scanning the shadowy expanse of the cavern.

GNOBEPCI8's sensors hummed. "These sound waves indicate movement from creatures endemic to this era. Their stature is approximately seven times our own, and their proximity makes their steps deafening."

Emerging from the transporter, the squadron's jaws dropped as they faced the towering creatures. They stood a thousand feet high, their immense forms radiating raw, primal power.

Attaka gasped. "I know these creatures. They're just like the ones that ravaged my home planet. If we stay still or play dead, they might ignore us."

GNOBEPCI8's metallic eyes glinted. "Such primitive beings are no match for our technology. I could eliminate them in a nanosecond with a laser beam."

Shadow Knight Warrior stepped forward, resolute. "Fear has no place here. Where I come from, Shadow Knights defend our villages against giants. We rely on courage, faith, and prayer."

The squadron nodded in silent agreement, carefully making their way through the cavern. But the calm didn't last long. A deafening roar echoed behind them, and a massive dinosaur charged at full speed.

"Run!" Attaka shouted, leading the way toward the pinnacle of a mountain visible through the cavern's entrance.

GNOBEPCI8 morphed into a sleek flying kite. "Get on!" he commanded.

One by one, the squadron leaped onto the kite as it soared upward, carrying them toward the mountaintop. But the dinosaur was relentless. It lunged, its massive jaws snapping inches from the kite.

The squadron braced themselves as the dinosaur's claws closed around them. Just as it seemed all hope was lost, GNOBEPCI8 activated the time machine. A blinding light erupted, pulling them out of the dinosaur's grasp and into the unknown.

Squadron lands in Pleistocene Era

The blinding light subsided, replaced by a stark, frozen landscape. The squadron found themselves atop a glacier, the icy expanse stretching endlessly in all directions. The air was frigid, biting at their skin as snowflakes swirled around them.

Iceberge's eyes widened as he took in the scene. "This... this feels like home. What year is this?"

GNOBEPCI8's voice remained steady despite the harsh cold. "We've arrived 11,700 years into the Pleistocene epoch.

"Welcome to the Ice Age" Iceberge said with his sparkled eyes. As the squadron adjusted to their surroundings, GNOBEPCI8 morphed once again, his body elongating and reshaping into a sleek ice slider. Without hesitation, the squadron climbed aboard, gripping tightly as the droid glided across the frozen terrain. The speed was exhilarating, the wind whipping past their faces as they sped through the icy world.

Suddenly, dark shapes emerged in the distance. They were ice creatures, their crystalline forms shimmering in the weak sunlight. Before the squadron could react, the creatures raised their icy limbs, unleashing a freezing wave that encased Shadow Knight Warrior, Attaka, and GNOBEPCI8 in solid ice.

Iceberge stood alone, unaffected by the freezing attack. His body, accustomed to the cold, allowed him to move freely. "Hang on!" he called, summoning his strength.

With a mighty blow, Iceberge shattered the ice encasing GNOBEPCI8. The droid immediately recalibrated, his mechanisms whirring to life. "Attaka, use your dragon flame!" GNOBEPCI8 instructed.

Attaka, still encased in ice, focused his energy. A faint glow began to emanate from within, growing stronger until flames erupted, melting the ice around him. Shadow Knight Warrior, though still frozen, whispered a prayer, and the warmth of his resolve shattered the icy prison holding him.

Together, the squadron launched a counterattack. Attaka's flames melted the creatures' frozen armor, while Iceberge's strength and GNOBEPCI8's precision dismantled their icy foes. Finally, the team stood victorious, but the glacier beneath them began to crack.

The ice gave way, plunging them into freezing water. GNOBEPCI8 wasted no time, morphing into an aquarium boat. "Climb aboard!" he urged. The squadron scrambled onto the boat as it stabilized on the churning waters.

As they drifted toward the shore, the water ahead erupted in a massive spray. A gigantic whale leaped from the depths, its gaping mouth hurtling toward the boat.

"Brace yourselves!" GNOBEPCI8 called out.

The whale's shadow loomed large over them, its jaws closing in. In a split second, GNOBEPCI8 activated the time machine once more. A luminous vortex enveloped the squadron, pulling them out of the Ice Age just as the whale's teeth grazed the boat's edge.

Squadron lands in Stone Age

The swirling vortex spat the squadron out onto solid ground, leaving them sprawled on a sandy shore. The air was thick and oppressively hot, a stark contrast to the frigid Ice Age they had just left behind.

GNOBEPCI8 retracted his aquatic form, returning to his humanoid droid shape. The squadron slowly got to their feet, brushing sand from their armor and taking in the surroundings.

A dense forest loomed nearby, its ancient trees standing as silent sentinels. Stones of varying sizes were scattered across the shore, and waves lapped rhythmically at the coastline. The sun blazed in the sky, its heat relentless and unforgiving.

"This heat... I feel like I'm melting," Iceberge groaned, visibly uncomfortable.

GNOBEPCI8 approached him, his mechanical hand extending into a laser-like apparatus. "Your body is acclimated to icy conditions, which makes you susceptible to extreme heat. Allow me to modify your wristband with ice immunity to counteract the effects."

A quick injection of energy into Iceberge's wristband brought immediate relief. He straightened, breathing easier as the oppressive heat no longer felt unbearable. "Thanks, GNOBEPCI8. That's much better."

Shadow Knight Warrior squinted at the horizon, his keen eyes scanning the terrain. "Where are we now? And what year is this?"

"We are in the year 8700 BCE," GNOBEPCI8 replied. "This is the early Stone Age, a time when human evolution was in its infancy."

The group fell silent, taking in the stark, primitive beauty of their surroundings. Shadow Knight Warrior's expression hardened. "This place feels ancient. It's as if time itself has forgotten it."

"Not entirely forgotten," GNOBEPCI8 interjected. His sensors whirred to life as he scanned the area. "My detectors have identified a local tribe nearby. Their movements suggest they are hunter-gatherers, potentially hostile if provoked. We must proceed with caution and avoid detection."

Attaka flexed his hands, his fiery spirit undeterred. "I'm ready for anything. If they want a fight, they'll get one."

Iceberge, still adjusting to the heat, shook his head. "If they're human, they might not be affected by ice. We need a different strategy."

Shadow Knight Warrior raised a calming hand. "Let us not rush into conflict. Peaceful diplomacy and prayer have been my weapons of choice for ages. Let's hope these tribesmen are willing to listen."

GNOBEPCI8 signaled for silence. "We move quietly from here. Follow my lead."

The squadron treaded cautiously along the island's shore, ears pricked at the faint rhythm of drumming and voices emanating from deeper within the jungle. They halted, ducking behind a broad, bushy tree as the sounds grew louder. Peering through the dense foliage, they caught their first glimpse of the local tribe.

Barefoot men with dark skin and primitive attire were gathered in a lively procession, their voices blending with the rhythmic beats of drums. They marched with purpose, pausing occasionally to chant. Fascinated, the squadron observed the tribe's way of life, noting their use of rudimentary tools and weapons.

GNOBEPCI8 activated his optical sensors, zooming in on their activities. The tribe hunted small birds and reptiles; their skills honed from generations of survival. Each hunter took turns consuming their modest catch, their camaraderie evident.

GNOBEPCI8 remarked quietly, "Their weapons — bows and arrows — are primitive and would not stand a chance against modern technology. Yet, they've thrived here for thousands of years."

Shadow Knight Warrior crossed his arms. "Surprised they've avoided droid invasions. We must be the first visitors from the future."

Iceberge smirked. "I could freeze their arrows before they even think of using them on us."

"Not advisable," GNOBEPCI8 said, his mechanical tone firm. "Interference could endanger them and disrupt our understanding of this era. Observation alone is sufficient."

The squadron nodded, agreeing to maintain their cover.

As the squadron remained hidden, a massive snail slid down the tree directly above them. GNOBEPCI8, always vigilant, zapped it with a precise laser beam. The shot obliterated the snail but also disintegrated the branch it clung to. The resulting crash startled the nearby tribesmen.

The tribe turned swiftly, spotting the squadron. Their leader barked orders in their native tongue, and arrows flew through the air toward GNOBEPCI8.

With calculated precision, GNOBEPCI8 neutralized the arrows mid-flight using laser beams. Iceberge froze another arrow before it could reach him, while Attaka unleashed a fiery breath that incinerated another projectile. Shadow Knight Warrior shattered an incoming arrow with a clean strike of his sword.

The tribe, overwhelmed by the squadron's technological prowess, retreated into the jungle.

"Follow them," GNOBEPCI8 instructed. "We must establish peace."

Deep into the jungle, the squadron found themselves surrounded. The entire tribe emerged from the foliage, bows drawn and aimed. GNOBEPCI8 quickly deployed a laser shield that deflected the barrage of arrows.

Realizing their weapons were ineffective, the tribesmen dropped to their knees, capitulating. GNOBEPCI8 deactivated the shield and stepped forward.

Using his advanced audio sensors, he played back fragments of the tribe's speech, piecing together their language. The tribesmen stared in astonishment as the droid communicated with them. Their leader hesitantly approached, exchanging words with GNOBEPCI8.

Attaka whispered, "That's incredible, GNOBE."

"By recording and analyzing their discourse, I found patterns to replicate their language," GNOBEPCI8 explained.

The tribe's leader shared their history — tales of survival in a harsh land and their enduring traditions. Shadow Knight Warrior looked thoughtful. "This knowledge might help us navigate back to our time."

The tribe invited the squadron to join them in a hunting expedition. GNOBEPCI8 stood among the gathered tribe, observing their struggles with hunting as they prepared for another arduous day.

Recognizing the opportunity to assist, he demonstrated his advanced capabilities. First, he retrieved a fallen bow and arrow, calculating the precise angle and force needed to strike multiple targets at once. Empowering the spear with his laser stealth energy, he transformed it into a dazzling projectile that emitted beams in multiple directions. With stunning precision and unimaginable speed, the spear struck several targets simultaneously, leaving the tribe and the squadron in awe.

The tribespeople erupted in cheers, their amazement reflected in wide smiles and grateful gestures. To show their appreciation, they placed offerings of gold and silver-stone at GNOBEPCI8's base, marvelling at his ability to revolutionize their hunting efforts and provide a bounty beyond their expectations.

As their time with the tribe drew to an end, GNOBEPCI8 announced the time machine's readiness.

"This place reminds me of hunting wolves back home," Attaka said wistfully.

"I've had enough of this heat," Iceberge muttered. "I'm ready to return to my icy domicile."

Before departing, Shadow Knight Warrior offers a prayer of protection for the tribe. The tribespeople, moved by the gesture, presented the squadron with a handcrafted souvenir. GNOBEPCI8 recorded the time period in his system as the squadron waved goodbye.

The tribespeople waved back, their expressions a mix of sadness and gratitude.

Squadron lands back in Base Portal

GNOBEPCI8 activated the time machine, setting the coordinates for the base portal. The transporter hummed to life, enveloping the squadron in a vortex of energy as they journeyed back to their original timeline.

Upon arrival, GNOBEPCI8 morphed back into his standard form.

Now, at the base portal, the squadron prepared for their ultimate return. GNOBEPCI8 recalibrated the time machine for individual departures.

Iceberge grinned. "Finally, I can return to where I belong."

Attaka echoed the sentiment. "It's been a journey, but I'm ready."

Shadow Knight Warrior placed a hand on GNOBEPCI8. "Thanks to you, I can reunite with my family."

The time machine hummed with power once again, and GNOBEPCI8, standing near the console, turned to the squadron.

"Who will be the first to return?" GNOBEPCI8 asked, his voice calm.

Shadow Knight Warrior stepped forward without hesitation. "I'll go," he said, his voice steady, though the faintest hint of sadness lingered in his tone.

GNOBEPCI8 nodded and adjusted the controls with precise movements. The machine responded, its mechanisms whirring as the destination year, **1270 AD**, appeared on the display.

"The machine is ready," GNOBEPCI8 said, stepping back.

Shadow Knight Warrior turned to face the group one last time. He looked at each of them—Attaka, Iceberge, and GNOBEPCI8—his eyes reflecting gratitude and sorrow.

"I'm going to miss you all," he said. "Thank you for everything, and especially you, GNOBEPCI8. I owe you more than I can ever repay."

Attaka stepped forward, raising his hand in a parting gesture. "Farewell, my brother. It was an honor to fight alongside you."

Iceberge followed, his voice warm with sincerity. "Goodbye, Warrior. Thanks for everything you've done—for all of us."

GNOBEPCI8 placed a reassuring hand on Shadow Knight Warrior's shoulder. "Go in peace," he said. "May you find what you're looking for when you return."

Shadow Knight Warrior offered a small smile, nodded, and stepped into the capsule. The lid slid closed with a soft hiss, enclosing him inside.

For a moment, the machine's hum grew louder, filling the room with a steady vibration. Then, with a sudden burst of light, it vanished—taking Shadow Knight Warrior back to his time.

CHAPTER 6
THE SECOND REVELATION

When the light faded, Shadow Knight Warrior found himself not in **1270 AD**, but in an unfamiliar yet hauntingly familiar place. He stood inside a grand monastery, its stone walls echoing the quiet murmurs of monks deep in prayer.

Confused, he glanced around. The air felt heavy with significance, as if the very fabric of time itself had shifted. He took a step forward, his armor clinking softly, and caught sight of the monks kneeling in reverence.

The sight stirred memories—distant, fragmented recollections of this very place. This was the monastery his family had visited long ago, a sacred space tied to his past.

A surge of emotion overtook him. Shadow Knight Warrior knelt down, placing his weapon carefully on the ground, and bowed his head in homage.

As he closed his eyes, a touch on his shoulder startled him. He turned quickly, his hand instinctively reaching for his weapon, but stopped when he saw the figure standing before him.

The man wore dazzling white robes that seemed to shimmer with an ethereal glow. His face was kind, yet firm, and his eyes bore a wisdom that transcended time itself.

"Hello, Shadow Knight Warrior," the man said, his voice steady and calm. "I am your grandfather. I've been sent here from the year 1050 AD to guide you."

Shadow Knight Warrior blinked in disbelief. "My grandfather?" he repeated, his voice barely above a whisper.

The man nodded. "Yes. I am the father of your father. I died over 500 years ago, but the time compression has brought me here for a reason. There is a divine mission ahead of you — one that ties together the past, the present, and the future."

Shadow Knight Warrior found himself lost for words. Sensing his resolve, the man's gaze softened, and he continued.

"The time compression has unraveled mysteries long buried, and now, it is time for you to know the truth. The vision you had this was not random. It came from the God of the Shadow Knights."

Shadow Knight Warrior's breath caught. "The God of the Shadow Knights? I've heard the legends, but…" He hesitated, searching for words. "How is this connected to me?"

His grandfather took a step closer, placing a hand on Shadow Knight Warrior's shoulder. "The Shadow Knights were not merely warriors; they were chosen by the divine to protect the balance of our world. You are part of this lineage — a dynasty that has worked for thousands of years to combat the forces of chaos." "A dynasty?" Shadow Knight Warrior echoed.

"Yes," the man affirmed. "Our family has been at the heart of this battle for centuries. But now, the stakes are higher than ever. The lost portal of Golaam has fallen into the hands of these forces. In the wrong hands, it has powers beyond our imagination."

Shadow Knight Warrior felt a chill run down his spine. "And this… divine mission?"

"You must rescue the portal," his grandfather said firmly. "The God of the Shadow Knights has entrusted you with this task. You have been chosen – you!" he said as he placed a hand on Shadow Knight Warrior's arm. Shadow Knight Warrior looked into his grandfather's eyes.

"What must I do?" he asked. The man smiled faintly. "That is the first step, my child. The rest will be revealed in time. For now, you must learn. Learn about what lies ahead."

Shadow Knight Warrior continued walking with his grandfather, an endless number of questions swirling in his mind.

"I'm not ready for this," he muttered, his voice trembling. "Why would the God of the Shadow Knights choose me? How do I know I'm even worthy of any of this?"

His grandfather placed a firm hand on his shoulder. "Doubt is natural, but it cannot stop you. The God of our dynasty does not make mistakes. You were chosen because you have the courage and the heart to carry this mission forward."

"But this enemy you speak of — these forces of chaos..." The Shadow Knight Warrior's voice faltered. "How can I fight things that are so powerful. How do I fight an enemy who controls time itself?"

His grandfather's expression darkened. "The one you are referring to is called Balrioch."

He sighed as he uttered the name.

"Balrioch is no ordinary foe. He was born in an orphanage in a distant world, his origins are mysterious to us. What we do know is that he was endowed with magical powers by alien forces, he has risen to lead a robotic world order. His droid army spans across time, compressing human-inhabited zones into chaos."

The Shadow Knight Warrior listened intently as his grandfather continued, detailing Balrioch's rise to power and his ultimate goal: the domination of all timelines. The time compressor, the device the Shadow Knight Warrior had glimpsed in his vision, was Balrioch's tool of destruction, bending time into an endless loop that trapped its victims.

"This conflict between the Shadow Knights and the Dark Knights began long ago," his grandfather explained. "Our dynasty stands for altruism and self-efficacy, while they thrive on chaos and domination. Balrioch is the culmination of their wickedness, a force unlike any we've faced before."

The Shadow Knight Warrior's heart grew heavy as his grandfather revealed the toll of time compression. A vision of his family crept into his mind, living in a fragmented past, their lives distorted by the unnatural loops of time.

"This is what's at stake," his grandfather said solemnly as if sensing his thoughts. "Not just your family, but the fate of all time-bound realms. To save them, you must stop Balrioch."

"But how can I face someone who exists in the future?"

His grandfather's eyes glimmered with resolve. "That is why I brought you here. To prepare you."

He led the Shadow Knight Warrior to a hidden chamber within the chapel, its walls decorated with ancient symbols. At the center of the room stood a closet, its heavy doors etched with intricate carvings. With a deliberate motion, the revenant opened the doors, revealing a dazzling sword resting within.

The Shadow Knight Warrior stared in awe. The blade looked as sharp as strands of hair and shimmered with a golden glow; its edges seemingly alive with divine energy.

"This," his grandfather said, "is the Shadow Knight Sword, the Sword of Judgment. For centuries, it has been reserved for the chosen one who would redeem our dynasty from its greatest threat."

"What makes it so special?"

"The sword bridges time itself," his grandfather explained. "Its power is invoked through prayer, but to use it fully, you must find another path. A way to synchronize Balrioch's time with ours. Only then can he be judged."

The Shadow Knight Warrior hesitated as his grandfather placed the sword in his hands. The blade felt impossibly light yet beaming with immense power.

"You won't face this challenge alone," his grandfather said. "The God of the Shadow Knights watches over you, and this sword will guide your way. Trust in your mission, and you will find the path forward."

The Shadow Knight Warrior tightened his grip on the sword, determination replacing his doubt.

"I'll do it," he said, his voice steady. "I'll stop Balrioch and restore the timeline. For my family, for our dynasty, and for all who suffer under this curse."

His grandfather smiled. "That is the spirit of a true Shadow Knight. Now, before you go, there are a few things left to do for you here."

The Shadow Knight Warrior was now led to an adjacent chamber. In the corner lay an old wooden chest. His grandfather gestured towards it. As he went over to open the chest, he realized that the chest was not an ordinary object. It was covered with intricate carvings indicating the work of a fine craftsman. He opened it and found clothes inside.

"Take off your attire and put these on," his grandfather commanded.

The Shadow Knight Warrior hesitated only for a moment before removing his battle-worn gear. The silver-metal attire within the chest glimmered, catching the faint light of the chapel. He lifted the pieces one by one, fastening them around his body. The armor fit perfectly, as though it had been forged specifically for him.

"Your path is clear, child," he heard his grandfather's voice from behind. "Strength lies not only in the blade but in faith and unity. Farewell."

Shadow Knight Warrior turned around only to find him alone in the assembly of monks. He wanted to say more to his grandfather but somehow, he knew that time with him was meant to be short-lived.

Determined to prepare for the challenges ahead, the Shadow Knight Warrior immersed himself in rigorous training under the guidance of monks. In their sanctuary, he learned to channel divine energy through focused prayer. With each session, his connection to the sacred power grew stronger.

The monks taught him to invoke judgment and holy energy, techniques that allowed him to unleash devastating strikes through his sword. Every movement became precise and calculated.

In another corner of the shrine, the virgins sang in a delicate harmony, their voices rising and falling like waves. The Shadow Knight Warrior joined them, his deep voice grounding their melody. Together, they prayed for angelic protection. Their combined song could be heard far beyond the chapel.

As their voices grew louder, the air around echoed. A radiant figure descended gracefully; its form illuminated with divine light. The angel touched the Shadow Knight Warrior's shoulder, and an overwhelming sense of peace and power washed over him.

"You are chosen," the angel whispered, its voice resonating in his mind.

A new specialty awakened within him — the ability to amplify the choir's prayers. The Shadow Knight Warrior led the choir in one final hymn, and their voices joined together in perfect harmony.

With the complete hymn, he drew his sword. It glowed faintly, as though infused with the same divine energy that coursed through his veins. Satisfied, he returned the blade to its sheath, ready for whatever lay ahead.

Without warning, a wormhole ripped through the air beside him. He knew, as did the monks, that his destination lay on the other side.

The Shadow Knight Warrior stepped forward without hesitation. The world around him blurred and twisted as the wormhole transported him across dimensions.

When he emerged, he found himself at the Squadron Base Portal. The familiar mechanics of the time machine filled the air as its lid closed behind him. He took a moment to steady himself, then turned to face the squad.

Shocks registered on their faces.

"Oh no!" GNOBEPCI8 exclaimed, his metallic voice laced with concern. "It must have failed to send you back."

"What is with the new look?" Attaka asked, his gaze sweeping over his transformed appearance.

The Shadow Knight Warrior took a deep breath, recounting his encounter with his grandfather and the revelations he had received. "My grandfather revealed the truth about the time compression. It is the work of a droid master from the future, a being who manipulates time to serve his new world order. The situation is worse than we imagined. If we don't act, he will gain full control."

"So, what do we do?" Attaka asked.

"There is no stopping," Iceberge said firmly. "We must find where the time compression is being held."

"Exactly!" GNOBEPCI8 chimed in. "Finding out where it is should now be our main priority."

The Shadow Knight Warrior looked around at his team. The path ahead was uncertain, but they knew what they had to do, what needed to be done to bring back the restoration of time.

CHAPTER 7
SQUADRON SEARCHES SOURCE OF TIME COMPRESSION

The squadron gathered around GNOBEPCI8 as he activated a hologram using the laser beam sensor embedded in his mechanical frame. A brilliant, three-dimensional map illuminated in front of their eyes, casting shimmering blue and green hues across their faces.

"This," GNOBEPCI8 began, his voice mechanical as usual, "is where we are currently — an island shore orbiting an unknown galaxy. We are approximately 700 light-years away from our planetary origin."

Shadow Knight Warrior stepped closer, his dark eyes scanning the technical details of the map. "Can you determine the time period of this galaxy relative to ours?"

GNOBEPCI8 paused, zooming in on the map. The hologram adjusted, revealing complicated patterns of celestial bodies, their paths interconnecting like a jigsaw puzzle. "This galaxy exists in the future — an unknown time. Without intervention, it would take us several solar years to reach it. However..." GNOBEPCI8 gestured toward a glowing vortex on the map, "...a wormhole linked to the time machine could reduce our journey to merely hours."

The squadron nodded in appreciation of GNOBEPCI8's work.

As the hologram faded, the team began preparations to leave the deserted island. Before stepping away, Shadow Knight Warrior approached GNOBEPCI8.

Shadow Knight Warrior learns how to activate Time Machine

"GNOBE," he said in an inquisitive tone, "can you teach me how to manipulate time using the time machine?"

GNOBEPCI8 tilted his head, the faint hum of his processors filling the silence. "What exactly do you wish to learn?"

Shadow Knight Warrior crossed his arms. "I need to know how to transport an enemy from the future back to the past. During my encounter with my grandfather, he revealed that an enemy from the future is responsible for this time compression. If I can manipulate the time machine to send him to the past, he can face judgment by a Shadow Knight of my dynasty."

"That's a bold strategy," GNOBEPCI8 replied. "However, to execute it successfully, you must have precise knowledge of the past timeline."

Shadow Knight Warrior nodded confidently. "I'm well-versed in the chronology of my dynasty. I just need to understand the mechanics of the time machine."

GNOBEPCI8 extended his metallic hand, shrinking the time machine until it fit snugly in his palm. "Watch closely."

With precision, GNOBEPCI8 demonstrated how to rotate the clock's hands, moving them both clockwise and counterclockwise to set specific time periods. "The lever," he explained, "controls the scale of the time shift, while the dial determines whether the target is sent to the past or future."

The Shadow Knight Warrior observed intently as his mind absorbed every detail. As GNOBEPCI8 re-scaled the time machine to its original size, he included the rest of the squad, guiding them on how to transport objects or beings across time.

Shadow Knight Warrior took the time machine into his hands. With guidance, he learned to freeze time in its tracks and shift it seamlessly to either the future or the past. The newfound knowledge felt like power coursing through him, a divine gift meant to fulfill his mission.

After the training concluded, Shadow Knight Warrior fell to his knees, bowing his head in deep prayer. His whispered words were a mix of gratitude and resolve, seeking strength for the challenges ahead.

As he stood up again, Shadow Knight Warrior turned to GNOBEPCI8, "Thank you, GNOBE. I believe this knowledge will prepare me for the divine mission ahead."

Before GNOBEPCI8 could respond, Iceberge stepped forward, "Remember, warrior, this mission isn't just yours — it's ours. You won't face this alone."

GNOBEPCI8 nodded, his mechanical optics glowing faintly. "Iceberge is correct. Defeating an enemy from the future requires teamwork and advanced preparation. You cannot do this alone. Only a droid like me, who also originates from the future, can provide the insights and assistance needed to confront this robotic world order."

Shadow Knight Warrior considered this for a moment before replying, "You're right. We must reach the future galaxy where this time compression originates. Whether it's occupied or not, we'll need to secure it and undo the warping of space-time that got us into this whole mess."

GNOBEPCI8 refurbishes the new Shadow Knight Sword

GNOBEPCI8's voice turned more measured. "There's one more thing you must prepare for before we journey to the future: your sword."

Shadow Knight Warrior unsheathed his ancestral weapon, its blade shimmering faintly in the dim light. "This sword was given to me by my grandfather. It's no ordinary weapon — it's a Shadow Knight Sword, a sacred blade imbued with the power of divine judgment. To unleash its full potential, I must enter a deep, prayerful state."

Attaka leaned closer, his expression was curious. "I've never seen anything like it before. What makes it so special?"

"It's not just a weapon," Shadow Knight Warrior explained. "It's a symbol of my dynasty's legacy. When wielded correctly, it can deliver judgment through divine intervention."

GNOBEPCI8 analyzed the sword with his laser beam, scanning its structure. "While its significance is undeniable, its medieval design lacks the strength needed against the future technology of the robotic world order."

Shadow Knight Warrior raised an eyebrow. "You know of this world order?"

GNOBEPCI8's tone grew somber. "Yes. The droids we've been battling are from the same era. They've aligned themselves with the robotic world order, whose goal is to compress all time. I was created in that era, but unlike them, I was programmed to assist human knights. There are few like me."

The room fell silent as GNOBEPCI8 continued, "Allow me to strengthen your sword. My laser beam can enhance its power, making it a formidable weapon against the technology of the future."

With a nod of agreement, Shadow Knight Warrior handed the sword to GNOBEPCI8. The droid extended his laser sensor, focusing a precise, glowing beam onto the blade. Sparks flew as the metal shifted, its edges refined and infused with a radiant energy. When the process was complete, the sword shimmered with a newfound glow.

Shadow Knight Warrior held the blade aloft, its weight familiar yet transformed. "Thank you, GNOBE. This will be the weapon I need to fulfill my mission," he said as he swung the sword around in the air and then sheathed it with a loud click.

The time had come to leave the island. The squadron gathered near the ship, their gear packed and their purpose clear.

Iceberge extended his fist, his voice steady. "We do this together, or not at all."

Attaka stepped forward, placing his fist over Iceberge's fist. "For unity and honor."

Shadow Knight Warrior joined them, his expression firm. "For the legacy of the Shadow Knights."

Finally, GNOBEPCI8 scaled his mechanical arm, adding his fist to the formation. "For the preservation of time itself."

At that moment, the squadron was more than a team — they were a family bound by blood, bones, and metal.

CHAPTER 8
SECOND JOURNEY TO AN UNKNOWN FUTURE

The squadron gathered near GNOBEPCI8, their anticipation palpable. The sleek, mechanical figure once again began its transformation, intricate panels shifting and merging with an almost unreal precision. GNOBEPCI8's form elongated and streamlined, morphing into a faster-than-light-speed transporter. The glow of energy surged as he activated his advanced accelerator, ready to propel them through the vast expanse of space-time.

"Strap in, everyone," GNOBEPCI8's voice resonated through the cabin. "We're about to cross 600 trillion miles per hour. Hold tight."

The squadron braced themselves as a bright pulse of light enveloped the transporter. With a burst of acceleration, they were thrust into the whirl of the time warp, where colors and dimensions bent and twisted around them. Their mission was clear: locate the source of the mysterious time compression.

Portals dotted the time warp like shimmering gateways, each leading to unknown realms. GNOBEPCI8 guided them through with precision, avoiding anomalies and gravitational traps.

"We're looking for patterns," Iceberge said, staring intently at the holographic map GNOBEPCI8 projected. "Anything that stands out."

"There," Shadow Knight Warrior pointed to a portal emitting faint energy ripples. "That's the one."

GNOBEPCI8 adjusted course, heading toward the portal. Just as they approached, an ominous hum filled the transporter.

From the edges of the portal, mechanical sentinels emerged. Guardian droids, sleek and relentless, surged toward the squadron at full speed. Their metallic bodies glinted with a strange light, as they moved with synchronization.

"Incoming!" Attaka shouted. "We're surrounded."

The transporter's cabin vibrated as GNOBEPCI8 unleashed a calculated counterattack. From his transponder, beams of concentrated energy erupted, striking the droids with precision. Each blast neutralized multiple adversaries, but the droids kept coming, their numbers seemingly endless.

"We need to break through," Iceberge said, gripping the edge of his seat.

GNOBEPCI8's energy blaster shifted to maximum output. With a sweeping motion, he created a temporary gap in the droids' formation.

"Hold on," GNOBEPCI8 announced, propelling the transporter through the opening. As they cleared the onslaught, the droids regrouped but were left behind, unable to match the transporter's speed.

The transporter slowed as they reached the new portal. GNOBEPCI8 morphed back into his original form, his systems recalibrating after the intense encounter. The squadron stepped out cautiously, greeted by an eerie silence. The portal's interior was a vast expanse filled with cyborg creatures and droids; their glowing eyes fixed on the intruders.

"Looks like they were expecting us," Shadow Knight Warrior muttered, drawing his weapon. The creatures charged, but the squadron fought back with determination, each member displaying the strength of their abilities. GNOBEPCI8 provided support, his blasters firing in controlled bursts to cover his team.

After a grueling battle, the squadron stood amidst the wreckage of their foes. GNOBEPCI8's sensors began to buzz.

"There's a signal," he said, opening a holographic display. "It's coming from the center of a nearby galaxy. The radiation levels are intense — gamma rays of unprecedented power. It could be a black hole, or something far more dangerous."

Shadow Knight Warrior's eyes narrowed. "Then that's where we're headed."

GNOBEPCI8 nodded, his mechanical arms adjusting the hologram's focus. "We'll have to move quickly. The path won't be easy."

Shadow Knight Warrior manipulates time through Prayer

As they prepared to continue, the squadron suddenly found themselves under attack once more, this time by teleporting droids. These new adversaries were faster and more advanced. Their laser beams cut through the air with deadly precision.

"They're trying to trap us," Iceberge yelled.

GNOBEPCI8 activated his shield power, creating a protective barrier around the team. Despite his efforts, the droids' numbers grew.

Realizing they were outnumbered, GNOBEPCI8 made a swift decision. "Hold on," he said, opening the time machine's portal. The entire squadron was ingested into the swirling vortex, with the droids following close behind.

Inside the time machine, chaos erupted. The droids attacked relentlessly, but GNOBEPCI8 accelerated through the wormhole, gripping the squadron members with his mechanical arms to keep them secure. As they neared the exit, GNOBEPCI8 closed the portal behind them, cutting off the pursuing droids.

They landed on solid ground, only to find themselves surrounded once more. This time, an army of droids awaited them.

The enemy leader, a droid of gigantic size, stepped forward. "You have nowhere to escape now. Surrender, or you all will be obliterated. Look at that droid over there. Get him. You have two options now: You will either exterminate these pathetic humans who you have been helping escape from their own demise and join us or get exterminated with them"

The minion droids surrounded GNOBEPCI8, capturing him in their mechanical arms. GNOBEPCI8 sadly looks at the rest of the squad, "Sorry! I am sorry to have failed you in this mission. They are going to have us all exterminated. Don't worry I will not let them touch a finger on any of you."

The droids responded together.

"Look at you. You traitor! You are a traitor to your own race. Why are you helping these humans?" they said in unison. As the squadron prepared for the worst, Shadow Knight Warrior goes into deep prayer. As Shadow Knight Warrior meditates on his sword, he enters into a trance. Suddenly, a blast of dazzling light appears from above descending toward the Shadow Knight Warrior. The light froze time, halting all the droids' movements.

The dazzling light touches the Shadow Knight Warrior and draws the Shadow Knight Sword toward it. An angel descends into the sword and emits dazzling rays of light into the time machine held by the droid. Suddenly, the time machine freezes the movement of everything present except the Shadow Knight Warrior. The sword descends toward the hand of the Shadow Knight Warrior, and he performs a 360-degree spin and slices every single enemy droid present with the refurbished sword. All enemy droids imminently vanish out of sight except for the squadron.

Time machine now unfreezes all previously halted motion, and the time resumes with the squadron staring in awe. Shadow Knight Warrior holds his sword high and begins shouting.

"It works! It finally works. My final prayer is now effective. At last, the God of the Shadow Knights has answered my plea and cry for deliverance. It was not me but rather the God of my dynasty who delivered us from these future scavengers."

GNOBEPCI8 nodded solemnly, "There must be something very special about your new sword. I did not notice that before, but this sword is more powerful than I thought. My laser beam stealth energy power and morphing ability was not enough to evade or contend against all those armies of droids. They had us besieged and were too powerful for us to escape from but somehow you have shown another side of yourself that I did not know of; you have now shown your true potential as a great knight. I am here for you and will never back down from anyone no matter how powerful they are."

Shadow Knight Warrior said, "Thank you GNOBE! You have helped me find the connection between past and future. I am now confident that I can help us contend against this future enemy."

Iceberge added, "If we can only find where this enemy is located, we can turn this whole mess around and finally restore our rightful place."

GNOBEPCI8 replied, "Well, since there are no more droids left to stop us now, we can continue following the signal from the hologram."

GNOBEPCI8 now activated his hologram, tracing the signal that would lead them to their next destination. His advanced computations mapped out the quickest route, but it felt as if a sense of unease had settled over the droid.

The challenges they had faced so far had only grown more intense, and for the first time, he questioned what awaited them at the end of their journey. Determined to keep his allies safe, he unleashed his laser beam stealth camouflage, rendering the entire squad invisible.

"This will only last for a short time," he warned firmly. "We must move quickly to find the lost portal before our cover fades." One by one, the members of the squad vanished from sight, their figures blending into the surroundings as they prepared to step into the unknown.

CHAPTER 9
RESCUE OF THE LOST PORTAL

GNOBEPCI8 activated the time machine, its mechanical core pulsating once again as the squadron was pulled inside. Unlike before, the droid did not rely on his morphed transporter; instead, the machine consumed them entirely, propelling them into the unknown.

In an instant, they emerged from the undefined time portal, arriving at the signaled region. But as they neared their destination, an urgent alarm blared from GNOBEPCI8's system. A spectacular ray of light, unlike anything they had ever encountered, erupted from the nearby galaxy, sending waves of gravitational force rippling through space.

The squadron barely had time to react before they were caught in its pull. Radiant beams scattered in all directions, illuminating the void with an almost divine brilliance. The sheer force of the anomaly disrupted their stealth camouflage, causing their forms to flicker into visibility.

As they struggled against the force, it became clear—they were being drawn toward something more perilous than they had anticipated. The sensation was eerily similar to the pull of a black hole, a force so powerful even GNOBEPCI8's propellor failed to counteract it.

Through the radiant chaos, they glimpsed something remarkable: an endless array of ticking clocks suspended in the void, each one pulsing with the rhythm of time itself. The squadron drifted closer, their movements no longer their own, as if the clocks were selecting them.

The wilful sacrifice of GNOBEPCI8

GNOBEPCI8 swiftly retracted the time machine into his mechanical hand, ensuring its safety as they spiraled toward the center of the anomaly. Before they could make sense of the phenomenon, the squadron was abruptly sucked into one of the clocks. The sensation of falling intensified, the light around them dissolved into a sharp geometric pattern.

When they finally regained their bearings, they found themselves trapped inside an entirely new space — a square trap portal, devoid of any obvious escape. They were now prisoners of time itself.

Towering above them stood a powerful guardian droid. Its gleaming metallic frame glinted with strange red-black light. Without hesitation, the droid launched a cosmic blast, aiming to eliminate the intruders before they could react. The squadron barely had time to register the incoming attack before GNOBEPCI8 detected the danger and sprang into action.

Transforming into a sleek, aero-dynamic rocket, GNOB-EPCI8 propelled himself forward, intercepting the destructive force before it could reach his allies. The impact was instantaneous, an explosion of cosmic energy surrounding him as he absorbed the blast. The squadron watched in horror as GNOBEPCI8's frame cracked under immense pressure. With his power systems failing, he turned toward Shadow Knight Warrior, his mechanical voice steady but laced with finality.

"GNOBE, you sacrificed your life for us," Shadow Knight Warrior said, his voice thick with emotion.

"I am programmed to sacrifice my life for good human knights such as you," GNOBEPCI8 responded, his systems flickering. "But… I regret to see the end of my journey with you and the rest of the squad." With a final surge of energy, he extended a small, glowing device toward Shadow Knight Warrior. "Take this. It will allow you to activate the time machine and enter the portal where the time compression is held."

Shadow Knight Warrior took the device with a solemn nod. "GNOBE, without your assistance, we surely would not have made it this far into the future. Thank you for all your help. I will remember you in my final prayer. May you rest in peace."

A piercing cry shattered the silence as Attaka collapsed to his knees, his grief pouring out in anguished wails. "GNOBE, noooooooooooooooo!" But the droid had already succumbed, his lifeless frame crumbling away, leaving only the lingering echoes of his final sacrifice.

The situation now pressed upon the squadron, but there was no time to grieve. Shadow Knight Warrior steadied himself, turning to the remaining members with renewed determination. "This is now our final chance to rescue the lost portal. Otherwise, we — and the fate of humanity — will stay submerged under this time warp. Let us now go after whoever is stopping us from returning to our past before it is too late."

Squadron battle against Sentinel Droid

A deep, mechanical voice boomed through space, cutting through the gravity of the moment. "You insolent fools and nomads! How dare you intrude into our dimension? You are detracting–our control over time. Forfeit now, or it all ends here."

The guardian master droid emerged from the smoke of the explosion, its glowing red eyes scanning the intruders with disdain. Shadow Knight Warrior stepped forward, "Never! I will never forfeit."

The remaining three members of the squadron tightened their stance, preparing for the inevitable clash. The guardian master droid radiated an aura of overwhelming power, but they would not back down. They had a strategy, a way to defeat this foe using their unique abilities. Shadow Knight Warrior's final prayer would be their key to victory.

As the battle began, the squadron fought with everything they had, channeling their strengths to counter the droid's relentless attacks. Shadow Knight Warrior screamed and a powerful blast unleashed from his sword that weakened the droid's time-manipulating abilities. Iceberge followed with a freezing shockwave, slowing the droid's movements, while Attaka, fueled by rage and sorrow, struck with a series of devastating energy slashes.

As the droid faltered, Shadow Knight Warrior thought of everything GNOBEPCI8 had done for them. Anger surging through his veins, he jumped and, with one final slash, slit the droid's core open, obliterating it into pieces.

CHAPTER 10
THE FINAL REVELATION

With the time machine given by GNOBEPCI8, Shadow Knight Warrior and the remaining members of the squadron stood before the square trap portal. Holding the device firmly, Shadow Knight Warrior activated it and the portal groaned in response, its barriers dissolved as the team was engulfed once more in blinding light.

As they materialized inside the portal, a sense of foreboding filled the air. The space was an immense void, endless and shifting. It was as if they were back in the void they had started from. Before the squadron could react, the ground beneath them trembled. A towering mech, gleaming with reinforced armor, emerged from the shadows. Iceberge stepped forward, analyzing the enemy with narrowed eyes.

"Another droid," Iceberge muttered, his fists clenched.

Shadow Knight Warrior, however, remained still, his eyes locked onto the mech. He could feel a strange presence radiating from within.

"No," he said grimly. "That's not just a droid. That's Balrioch. Balrioch is the name revealed to me first in the vision, then by my grandfather. The mystery is now revealed. This must be the final revelation."

The realization sent a wave of tension through the squadron. The mastermind behind the time warps, the architect of destruction, stood before them in an armored, mechanical disguise.

"Then we take him down now," Attaka declared, his voice filled with fury over GNOBEPCI8's sacrifice.

The battle erupted in an instant. The squadron launched a combined assault, utilizing every ounce of strength they had left. Iceberge unleashed torrents of ice, freezing the air around Balrioch's mech, while Attaka struck with powerful shockwaves. Shadow Knight Warrior wielded the energy of the Shadow Knights, his final prayer echoing through the void, but the mech's armor absorbed it, rendering the sacred power ineffective.

Balrioch retaliated with calculated precision, firing beams of concentrated energy that split the battlefield apart. The squadron was forced into a desperate struggle, dodging and countering with all their might. It was only through synchronized effort, relentless attacks, and sheer determination that they managed to exploit a weakness in the mech's structure. Shadow Knight Warrior, seizing the moment, drove his blade into the mech's core, igniting a chain reaction within.

With a deafening explosion, the mechanical shell of Balrioch crumbled. The squadron braced themselves, watching as the smoke cleared. Had they finally ridden themselves of the menace that had plagued their mission? Was it really true?

Alas…

From the ruins of Balrioch's mech, a spectral force erupts, freezing both Iceberge and Attaka in place. The esoteric beams glow an eerie blue, crackling with energy before encasing them in shimmering orbs. In a flash, they vanished, transported into the void beyond the battlefield.

"Attaka! Iceberge! Noooooooooooooooo!" Shadow Knight Warrior's voice echoes through the void as he watches helplessly. Attaka's final words ring in his ears: "Warrior, we are counting on you."

Darkness engulfs him. The battlefield disappears, replaced by a cold and silent void. He stands alone in the shadowy dimension, an endless expanse of floating time spheres. Each sphere contains faces from his past — loved ones lost to the flow of time. Their voices murmur around him, whispering his name, pleading for his help.

His despair deepens. "I'm tired of all this. I want to go back home. I just want to be with my family again." His cries are swallowed by the void, his strength wavering. But then, from within one of the glowing spheres, a familiar voice calls out.

"My son, in order to return to the past and be with your family again, you must defeat him. Remember, make your final prayer. You are now the only hope of the lost world."

It is his grandfather, the wise figure from the monastery portal. His words reignite a fire within Shadow Knight Warrior's heart. He clenches his fists, determination replacing sorrow.

The Final Prayer of Shadow Knight Warrior

Without warning, a blinding vortex engulfs him, hurling him through a faster-than-light time capsule. Time itself bends and twists around him as he is pulled into the very core of the time compressor. The void shifts, revealing a grand, ominous structure pulsating with streams of ticking clocks. In its center, Balrioch emerges in his true form — a being of pure darkness carrying with his hand the time compressor.

"I am Balrioch, ruler of all space-time. You have intruded into a realm beyond eternity of which I control. You will now remain forever lost, beyond the point of no return."

Shadow Knight Warrior tightens his grip on his new sword. His final prayer begins. Divine energy courses through him, illuminating the abyss with a radiant glow. The power of his ancestors flows into his blade. At the peak of his prayer, he activates the time machine, locking Balrioch's existence with that of an ancient past.

Time shatters.

A colossal force pulls Balrioch backwards in time. He is transported to the medieval age. The Shadow Knights, summoned through Shadow Knight Warrior's final prayer, passes judgment on him.

As Balrioch receives judgment, Shadow Knight Warrior jumps up and thrusts both sword and time machine directly toward the center of the time-compressor. As both the sword and time clock plunge into the event horizon, the time machine of the square trap portal comes to a halt. The time machine comes to a complete halt and reverses direction of time clocks at rapid speed causing them to implode.

As the Shadow Knights begin to pronounce judgment on Balrioch, Balrioch camouflages himself using dark knight magic powers. This clever tactic of Balrioch makes him invincible to the sword of the Shadow Knights, but not necessarily to prayer. As the Shadow Knights lose track of Balrioch, they begin engaging in deep prayer. Balrioch attempts to escape back into the wormhole that brought him into the medieval age, but Shadow Knight Warrior has already unleashed the time compressor by plunging both his Shadow Knight Sword and time clock into the event horizon. Balrioch attempts to desperately cling to the time-compressor using his dark knight magic prowess, but it diverges away from him.

With a startling countenance, Balrioch has come to the realization that his now defeated robotic world order is no longer able to aid him. Balrioch is seen helplessly clasping his elongated hands to once again gain access to the time-compressor but loses complete power and is instead sucked back into the time machine initiated by the Shadow Knight Warrior's final prayer to receive his judgment.

As the Shadow Knights persist in prayer, shadowy forces begin to engulf Balrioch, plunging him into an inescapable corner where he begins to gradually obliterate into darkness. As a result, Balrioch loses all control and power over time and is no longer able to compress it.

Shadow Knight Warrior stands exhaustively in his position, gasping for air. Suddenly, out of the energy leak of the timeclocks comes the formation of a new wormhole. The time-compressor starts releasing all time-spheres to the wormhole. The time-compressor releases small bubbles containing living entities that were trapped and compressed inside of it. Time-spheres are seen diverging away from the time-compressor and gravitating toward the wormhole.

Shadow Knight Warrior continues to gasp while glaring at the spectrum of time-spheres moving toward the wormhole from the cosmic warp. The time-compressor begins to dissolve as all the time-spheres are released from it. The sword and time clock of the Shadow Knight Warrior that he thrust into the center of the time-compressor returns to him in a sudden gale. Shadow Knight Warrior suddenly gets transported to the opening wormhole that takes him back to his past.

CHAPTER 11
RETURN TO THE PAST

His feet touched solid ground, and as he looked around, he found himself in a familiar setting — the dining room of his family home in Golaam. The room had changed, aged with time, but its essence remained the same. His heart pounded as he turned toward the corner, where an elderly woman stood, staring at him in disbelief.

"Mother, is that you?" Shadow Knight Warrior's voice was laced with wonder and hesitation.

The matron gasped, stepping forward, tears welling in her aged eyes. "Oh my God. Shadow? Where have you been? It has been over fifty years since we last saw you."

He took a step closer, absorbing the lines of age that had deepened on her face. "It does not seem like it has been fifty years. You look different… You have aged tremendously."

His mother's hands trembled as she reached out to touch his face, ensuring he was real. "I have been heartbroken for the past fifty years, mourning my lost son."

"I don't know what happened to me. I was transported through time and landed in the future. There, I met these alien creatures with advanced technology and supernatural abilities. They had descended upon the past, disrupting our space-time. I was chosen to deliver you and the rest of the lost world from this time compression." He paused, his voice heavy with the weight of his experiences. "It was an ordeal… but I am glad it is finally over."

His mother nodded solemnly, fresh tears escaping down her wrinkled cheeks. "You are not the only one who suffered. I endured fifty years of pain, wondering if I would ever see you again. I cried out to the God of Golaam, asking why this happened to our only son. We have been praying for you to return."

Shadow Knight Warrior placed a reassuring hand on her shoulder. "Your prayers have been answered."

She studied his face, noting the absence of any signs of aging. "This time travel… it has frozen you in time. You look exactly the same from the day you vanished."

Before he could respond, the sound of footsteps approached. His father and younger sister entered the room, their faces lined with years of longing. His father stopped in his tracks, eyes wide in shock. "Welcome back, son. My God… you still look the same. Fifty years have passed, yet you remain untouched by time."

His younger sister, now appearing older than him, stepped forward hesitantly. "Shadow? Is it really you?"

"It's me," he assured, his voice filled with emotion.

They embraced him, their collective warmth grounding him in the reality of the moment. When they finally pulled away, Shadow Knight Warrior reached for the sword at his side. He unsheathed it, its blade gleaming with a brilliance beyond time.

"I brought this back with me," he said, offering the sword to his father. "A souvenir from the future."

His father took it reverently, admiring the craftsmanship. "It's magnificent…"

Then, Shadow Knight Warrior pulled out the time machine, the device that had made his journey possible. The family gasped at its intricate design, eyes wide with awe.

"What is that?" his father asked.

"A gift from the future," Shadow Knight Warrior replied, placing it on the table.

His father's eyes shimmered with pride. "You truly are the Shadow Knight Warrior."

Tears welled in the old man's eyes as he pulled his son into an embrace. The weight of decades apart dissolved into the warmth of their reunion.

In the days that followed, the family made a pilgrimage to the monastery. There, they offered prayers of gratitude, celebrating Shadow Knight Warrior's divine accomplishment. The people of Golaam recognized his role in restoring the balance of time and freeing those who had been trapped.

Back at the family home, the sword was placed atop a cabinet, a symbol of honor and triumph. Nearby, a ticking clock hung on a hook, its steady rhythm marking the passage of time—uninterrupted, unbroken, and finally at peace. Shadow Knight Warrior gazed at it for a moment before closing his eyes, allowing himself to rest at last. His journey was over.